A STORY ONLY FATE COULD TELL

Mac Chestnut

JUNE 1, 2026
CHESTNUT PUBLISHING
Mineral Wells, TX

This is a work of fiction. Names, characters, places, and incidents are the product of the author's imagination or are used fictitiously. Any resemblance to actual persons, living or dead, events, or locales is entirely coincidental.

ISBN: 979-8-9959717-0-2 (Paperback Edition)
ISBN: 979-8-9959717-1-9 (eBook Edition)

Library of Congress Control Number:

2026911543

Acknowledgements

The literary journal, The First Line, inspired this novel. Each year, the editors offer four first lines and challenge authors to write a short story beginning with each quarter's prompt. As an extra challenge, writers are encouraged to write a four-part story using all of the first lines for that year. This challenge is issued in December, and all submissions are due on the first of February.

Being a novice writer, I thought I was up to that challenge and feverishly went to work. Though *A Story Only Fate Could Tell* was not selected, a kind note about the story's main character from David LaBounty, the journal's editor, gave this writer the encouragement to keep writing.

This story sat on the shelf for two years before I decided to return to it. After much editing and rewriting, I realized why I did not make the grade. I have a degree in music, not grammar. Special thanks to Elizabeth Oliver for her editing prowess.

A special thanks to my wife, who has heard this story too many times to count.

Lastly, thank you for reading my story. I hope you receive as much joy from this tale as I did telling it.

To Dana Leigh, my soul mate

Part One

1

Mr. Morton needed a new pair of shoes. The once blemish-free leather was peeling at the toes and heels, the stitching was frayed, and the mirrorlike spit shine distorted reflections like a trick mirror in a carnival funhouse.

As he slipped the shoes onto his feet, right foot, left foot, Mr. Morton looked up at the over-laden bookshelves that flanked the brick hearth in his living room. In the center of the solid oak Shaker-style mantel, a child-sized baseball glove, stained with the effects of time and the buildup of soot, sat alone.

Some objects are too precious for any human to discard, despite their age or condition. These semi-sacred objects become talismans of memory, a temporal flash drive, holding onto the past until its memories are revisited on purpose or by happenstance. Mr. Morton's shoes were neither, and they were both. It was difficult to explain, even for a gifted diviner of oration like Mr. Morton.

The soot-stained glove and worn-out shoes did not contain expertly crafted prose, unforgettable characters, or poetically illustrated worlds, but beneath the dust and wear lay a story only fate could tell. It was Mr. Morton's story, it was Allie's story, and he knew Allie was born to write it.

***

Allie stood at the stovetop over a skillet of bacon and eggs, wearing an apron over her lavender surgical scrubs. She stepped back from the range with a spatula in her hand and craned her head down the hallway. "Wake up, Stan. For goodness' sake, you're going to be late on the first day."

"Just a minute, Mom. I'm up," Stan answered from behind the closed bathroom door.

"Sorry. Thought you were still asleep," exclaimed Allie as she placed two over-easy eggs and three slices of bacon onto the plate alongside four neatly cut wedges of buttered toast. Allie didn't cook like this every morning, but a warrior's breakfast on the first day of school was a family tradition.

Over the past year, making sure Allie's little soldier had a full stomach was as useless as mowing the yard. The grass always grew back, and Stan was always hungry.

"Morning, Mom!"

Stan took his seat at the table and looked out the window into the backyard, hoping to see something he knew had escaped his memory. As soon as Allie set his breakfast on the table, Stan began devouring the feast like a messy soldier shoving his disheveled uniforms into his footlocker moments before inspection.

"Coffee?" Allie asked as she filled her mug that read "Best Mom Ever."

"Gross!" grunted Stan, never looking up from his breakfast.

Allie let out three giggles followed by a quick snort.

"Now that I know you're awake, are you excited about your first day of junior high?"

"Yeah, I guess so," answered Stan, focused intently on what remained of the crispy bacon.

Allie grinned. “You guess so? Come on. You’ve got to be feeling something other than ‘I guess so.’”

“I mean, it’s just another school year, Mom. Nothing to get all worked up about,” replied Stan before devouring every edible thing he could get his hands on.

Allie took in a deep breath and a familiar scent wafted from her elegant nose into her cerebral cortex, and everything in her told her something that she knew was impossible. She smelled her Jimmy. Taken aback, Allie’s eyes focused, her chin rose toward her left shoulder, and her eyebrows pulled tight toward her soft but defined cheekbones. “Are you wearing cologne?”

“Yeah, I borrowed some of Dad’s.” Stan targeted the eggs.

A gentle smile spread across her full lips. She breathed in the familiar scent, and the tension in her shoulders melted away. “Does that mean you used deodorant, too?”

“All I could find was yours. It’s a little girly and smells like baby powder. Can I get my own?” asked Stan.

Allie set her right elbow on the table, rested her chin on her open palm, and looked into the face of her baby boy. The polaroid of memory snapped an image of the boy she knew was racing toward manhood at a pace she would slow if she could.

"Sure we can, Stan the Man."

Stan's caloric intake halted, and he looked up. "Mom, please don't call me that around my friends. Promise?"

The corners of Allie's mouth drew downward and her eyes rolled slightly upward before resting back on her son. She asked, "What's wrong with Stan the Man?"

Momentarily diverted from his breakfast, Stan explained, "Nothing's wrong with it, except I'm not a little kid anymore. You didn't notice, but I shaved this morning, too!" He turned his face from left to right, revealing two bits of toilet paper clinging to his left cheek and chubby chin by minuscule splotches of crimson.

"Oh, my goodness, you cut yourself." Allie stood, walked around the table, gently grabbed Stan by the chin, and gasped. "Lemme look?"

Allie raised her left eyebrow. "Honey, what razor did you use?"

"The one in the bathtub."

Allie's eyes closed, and her head involuntarily swung from left to right.

"When we buy deodorant, can I get my own razor? Using your mom's is kind of gross." Stan grabbed a few bits of bacon and a wedge of toast, shoving both into his mouth as if he knew somehow they would fit. Which they did, but just barely.

"That's nasty, Stan. Now I'm going to need a new razor, too." Allie began to laugh, which meant she also snorted.

"That's how I always know it's real."

"What's real?"

"Your laugh. When it's not fake, you snort." Muffled by the mouthful of what had been on his plate moments before, it sounded more like, "Wor waf. Fwen it's fnaht fehk, few shnort."

"All right, Stan the Man, don't talk with your mouth full, and what does it mean when I don't…" she paused, then made the snorting sound.

Stan laughed and turned to his left, holding his ribs. "Stop it, Mom. Don't get me laughing before I even get to school. Do you know how much trouble I'll be in if I laugh when Ms. Singleton starts pointing to her whiteboard with that nub she has for an arm?"

"Stanley Lane, that's horrible!" Her inner eyebrows furled down toward her nose, creating a V shape whose invisible subtitle read "Stan is in trouble." Allie held the stern mother look that always accompanied her use of Stan's middle name as long as she could. Stan exercised all the discipline in his pubescent body to stifle his laugh. Then, Allie snorted. Laughter, snorts, and the grabbing of ribs ensued. Allie's pale auburn ponytail swung around her head like an airplane propeller. Stan doubled over, his stomach burning with exertion, and his fists worked wrinkles into his T-shirt that read "Sarcasm Is How I Give Hugs."

"Stop it. Stop it, Mom. This is supposed to be serious. As Mr. Perkins always says," Stan dropped into as deep a voice as he could muster, "this…is…school. We are not here to have fun!" His voice cracked on the word fun, which made

Allie snort and Stan add a few more wrinkles to that T-shirt he thought was so funny but Allie found tacky. It was a battle she chose not to fight, as all parents must do or learn from their folly.

When Allie stopped snorting, Stan caught his breath. Allie broke the silence. "Wanna pray?"

"Absolutely." Stan closed his eyes and made an *Ohm* sound like a Buddhist monk meditating and brought his hands together in a choreographed motion that looked more like a martial arts move than a sign of devout conformity. When he opened his eyes, Allie reached across the table with outstretched hands. With hands entwined over the remnants of breakfast, Allie and Stan recited the Lord's Prayer. Though not a Baptist tradition, the Lord's Prayer was the most she could ever muster outside church.

"Amen," they echoed in unison.

Stan stood, cleared the table, rinsed the dishes and silverware at the sink, and placed them in the dishwasher. Looking over his shoulder as he wiped down the counter, he asked, "Why do we always say the Lord's Prayer?"

Allie looked down, touched the diamond ring on her left hand, and professed, "If that prayer was enough for Jesus, it ought to be enough for us."

Allie watched Stan gather his backpack and sling it over his shoulder and savored the last sip of her morning coffee. The realization that Stan would not be her little boy for much longer lay heavy on Allie, but she knew all too well that kids grow up and parents grow old. Fate was driving that train full speed ahead, and she was just a passenger enjoying these small slices of contentment when she could.

Looking through the window out over the backyard, Allie's most sacred memory played out like a silent picture show. The ghost of better times faded, reality came into focus, and Allie added clean windows to her never-ending to-do list. She looked down and realized she was rubbing her wedding band.

Stan walked up behind her, placed his hand on her shoulder, and asked, "Can I ride with you today?"

Her inner mom's heart fluttered, and Allie felt the temperature rise in her cheeks. "Stan the Man can ride with me any day."

"Mom," he admonished, rolling his eyes, "you promised not to call me that in front of my friends."

"I know. Just getting it out of my system, Stan the Man. Let me grab my keys."

Allie and Stan went out the back door and walked toward the blue sedan parked at the end of the driveway just in front of the garage. Allie rocked into him, knocking him off balance just enough to make him giggle.

Rocking back into her, he beamed and said, "I love you, Mom."

"I love you, Stan the Man."

Allie backed the car out of the driveway, drove down Maple Street, and entered the queue of cars waiting in the drop-off lane. There were few certainties in Appledale. However, finding Mr. Morton standing atop the steps beneath the Appledale Junior High School flagpole was as sure as betting on Alabama to win on any given fall Saturday. If school was in session, Mr. Morton was there, greeting each student with a fist bump or a high five.

Allie waved to the elderly man in a tweed jacket with elbow patches and nodded. "Aw, Mr.

Morton is the best. I hope you are in his class, Stan. You'd love it."

"He's my last class of the day."

Allie beamed. "It's going to be a great year for you, Stan the Man."

Stan complained, "Mom, I thought we had a deal?" Then he reached across the console for the conciliatory hug she wasn't expecting.

"Well, isn't this just the best morning ever?" Allie exclaimed with a smile only a parent could recognize. Stan opened the door and bounced up the steps toward the school.

As she began to pull away, she saw Mr. Morton hurrying down the steps like a man half his age. Allie pulled to a stop and rolled down the passenger side window as the aged professor leaned down with wide eyes and ears pulled up by the grin he couldn't quite contain.

"Is that the same Allie that sat three seats back in the third row, lost as a white kitten in a blizzard?"

"It sure is. Wow, I can't believe you remember that. It's been what, fifteen years?"

"Nineteen if we're annotating footnotes. How could I forget Allie's ability to weave a tale?"

"That's amazing that you remember me. You've had hundreds of kids in your classes over the past, how many years now?"

"Forty-eight years teaching, or at least trying to. Only forty-one in Appledale. Still a rookie around here. I guess it's time to retire when the offspring of your former scholars start showing up in class, but I don't see myself quitting anytime soon. Still love it."

"These kids are lucky to have you, Mr. Morton. Can I buy you a cup of coffee and catch up?"

He shook his head. "Of course not!"

"I'm sorry. I meant no offense."

"Oh, Allie. I'm not offended. You're a busy woman raising a kid, and I can't let you buy me a cup of coffee. But I'd be happy to buy you one."

"You're as chivalrous as I remember. Let me get your number, and I'll text you mine." Allie took her cell phone out of its dashboard cradle.

"Text?" Mr. Morton rolled his eyes and chuckled. "Why don't you just call me this evening?"

"Sure. I can do that. What's your number?"

Allie entered his number into her contacts, listing his first name as "Mr." and his last name as "Morton."

"Well, Allie, if this hasn't been the most enjoyable morning in a long time."

"I just told Stan the same thing."

"Stan? I have a Stan McDermitt in my last class," Mr. Morton remarked, scratching the beard that had faded to brilliant silver. "Oh, how wonderful." He shook his head, grinned, and giggled. "This makes an old man's heart happy." Mr. Morton's smile faded, and he hesitated. "I think about you and Jimmy often."

"We met in your…"

Allie's response was cut short by a loud honk from the car waiting behind her. Even a town as small as Appledale had an asshole, and she was living up to her reputation.

Mr. Morton shook his finger at the impatient driver and spouted, "Glad to see you're still so patient and considerate, Esther Borden." The aged shaper of thoughts and dreams leaned back down, his face swinging left and right in pure joy. "Give me a call. We'll catch up, Allie. I'll make sure Stan is taken care of. As for our dear scholar Esther Borden, they're born every day."

"I think it's Esther Peabody now."

Mr. Morton frowned. "Well, then their children are at a serious genetic disadvantage."

Allie laughed with a snort. Mrs. Peabody threw them both the international peace sign, and Allie noticed the worn-out shoes on Mr. Morton's feet as he marched back to his morning post. With a friendlier wave, Allie acknowledged Esther, put the car in drive, and made her way to Wanda's for one more cup of coffee.

There wasn't an empty seat at the counter. So, Allie walked to the table in the back corner of Dixon's Diner. The eatery was what one expected when they thought of a small town café: specials written on a chalkboard above the service window, old men in straw hats (because even in Appledale they knew not to wear a felt hat until after Labor Day), the smell of fried bacon, and a wiry, strong-jawed woman giving hell right back at Mr. Wilson.

"Don't look at me like I owe you money, Bobby Wilson. I'll shove my boot so far up your crotchety old ass, I'll spit shine it with your damn tongue."

The group of men that gathered every morning erupted in laughter. Pastor Don's face winced in shock, and the sight of that made Allie snort again.

"Pastor, don't you look at me like that. Jesus had to kick a little ass, too, if I remember correctly." Wanda fired at the young minister.

"Yeah, but Jesus never pretended to be a proctologist," quipped the pastor.

"That's right, ophthalmologist and a sommelier were more his speed. But you leave that last one out of your sermons. Don't ya, Preacher?"

Old man Wilson turned and pleaded, "Turn the other cheek, Pastor. Trust me on this one."

"Y'all cut your shit. There's a lady in here, and it ain't me." Wanda sauntered to Allie's table with a cup of coffee, a stainless steel container of cream, and three sugar cubes. "Here you are, honey. Just like you like it." Wanda sat in the chair across from Allie.

"Morning, Wanda. See you're in top form today." She dropped the three cubes of sweetness into the dark black liquid, stirred, and slowly added the cream until the steaming liquid turned the color of buffed leather.

"Honey, with these assholes, you always have to be in top form. You eatin'?"

"No, ma'am. It's Stan's first day of school, so I cooked eggs and bacon for him and even some for myself."

Wanda joked, "I didn't hear any fire trucks, so I guess that went well."

"It's been a fine morning. I especially enjoyed that boot up your ass line. That original?"

"Hell, no. Read it in a Jack Reacher novel. Made up the spit shine with your tongue bit," Wanda confessed, her lips peeling upward in an 'I got that asshole, didn't I' smirk.

"You think the preacher even knows what a sommelier is?" asked Allie, pointing over at Pastor Don.

"Doubt it. You know he's Baptist, right?"

"I hope so. I go to his church every Sunday."

"What the hell for?"

"Why the hell not?" Allie's eyes focused, and a laser beam of stubbornness caused a crack in Wanda's normally stoic facade.

Wanda attested, "I go twice a year. As long as a Baptist I know dies." She held out her fist toward the backside of the clergyman, curled up her middle finger, followed by her pointer, and added, "Twice."

"What's wrong with Baptists?" asked Allie, unsure she wanted to hear the answer.

"Nothing, I guess. Except they all think they've got it right, and the rest of us are just unblessed by God himself, unworthy of his bountiful grace and unending good nature." Wanda made a large circle around her head. The circle became a mimed noose, which Wanda pulled, causing her head to tilt sideways and her tongue to hang out of her mouth. Her eyes rolling up in the back of her head was an added extra.

Allie took her notebook from her purse, placed her folded hands on its cover, and remarked, "Don't be so dramatic. The church wasn't made for perfect people."

"Tell that to Beaulah. She sure thinks she's perfect."

"And that is exactly why she isn't. You should come with me next Sunday. Stan is reading the scripture."

"The one about burning the old cussing witches at the stake?"

Allie shrugged and rolled her eyes. "We save that one for Sunday nights. If you come then, you have to bring your own chicken."

"A chicken?" Wanda sat up straight, eyebrows creased in curiosity.

"For the blood sacrifice, of course."

"Cut your shit, Allie." Wanda leaned forward and placed her elbows on the table, cradling her chin with open palms. "That was a good one. So, how many years have you been writing this story you won't let nobody read?" she asked, pointing at the notebook.

"I don't know." Allie took a long sip of her coffee and set the cup on the table. Her eyes swung upward. She inhaled, tilted her head upward, and tapped her pen on the unopened journal. "That's not true. Every story I've ever written started in Mr. Morton's class."

Wanda shrugged. "He's too old to be teaching those brats. I told him so, but he's stubborn as hell."

"I didn't know you two knew each other."

Wanda wiped the table with her dish towel and rearranged the napkin holder. “It’s a small town, and this is the only café. Everybody has to eat out sometime.”

Allie leaned forward. “Really? And how often does Mr. Morton come by?”

“As often as he gets hungry. Like everybody else around here.”

“I think he should teach as long as he still loves doing it. The kids love him.”

“Yeah, they do. The new principal, not so much, but that kid wasn’t even a wet dream when Lee Morton got his master’s degree from Boston University.”

“I never understood how a man like Mr. Morton ended up in this one-horse town.”

“Same reasons as the rest of us, honey. We either love it, or we’re too chickenshit to leave.”

“Or maybe, it’s just home.”

“That’s the truth.” Wanda shook her head yes and no at the same time. “It’s just home.”

Allie sipped her coffee, and Wanda wiped the already clean table.

“How many stories have you written?” asked Wanda.

"Too many to count and none worth reading." Allie slumped back into the chair and relaxed her shoulders.

"I'd read them. It's better than standing over at the counter, wondering what the hell you're writing in that little brown book of yours."

The bell on the diner's door chimed, and a man of average height but very unaverage looks entered in a well-fitted suit, a tie flung over his left shoulder, and carrying a black leather folio. Wanda watched Allie intently. Allie's eyes quickly danced toward her folded hands, which unfolded and raced under the table and into her lap.

When Allie looked up, Wanda's left eye squinted in contrast to her looming right eye, her mouth pursed, and the fierceness of both pulled the tip of her nose down. "Now, that is a fine specimen of man right there."

Allie looked into her cup of joe. "I didn't notice."

"Are you blind? I'm older than Moses and hell, and I can see how fine that man is. You should talk to him."

Allie reached for her spoon and stirred her already perfectly mixed coffee. "He's a nice man, but who I talk to isn't anyone's business."

Wanda whispered, "Allie McDermitt, you have a secret," then leaned forward, waiting for a response.

"There are no secrets in this damn town. Now, mind your own business." Allie sat back, forehead wrinkled, and awaited Wanda's almost certain verbal uppercut.

"Well, well, well. Allie McDermitt. Glad you finally knocked the dust off that old cat." Wanda swung her towel softly over Allie's face, which was as red, as Wanda would say, as a baboon's backside. The old waitress made a *tsk, tsk, tsk* sound and leaned over the table. "Everybody in this town has a secret."

"And you know all of them, don't you?"

"Most of them, and the ones I don't, nosy old Beaulah does."

"You're right about that. You two know all the tea and spill it every chance you get."

"Ain't nothing wrong with it, honey."

"Wrong with what? Spilling the tea?"

"No, I'm pretty sure that gossiping is a sin, but curing loneliness ain't."

"Who said I was lonely?"

"I do. Listen! Contrary to Pastor Don's naive nature, everyone in this town is fucking somebody. If not, you can be sure they fuck themselves."

Allie tried to hold it in, but couldn't. A muted giggle followed by unstifled snorts turned every head in the diner.

"You are awful," Allie exclaimed.

"Awfully right."

Allie caught her breath, and Wanda returned to the counter and refilled Pastor Don's coffee. She made sure not to spill any on his open Bible.

The well-dressed attorney smiled at Allie from across the room, and her cheeks flushed with color. She took the pen in hand, scribbled a note, and carefully tore it out of her book of secrets. Allie placed the pen and book back in her oversized purse, put a worn five-dollar bill under the empty coffee cup, and walked toward the exit. She passed the table where the handsome gentleman sat and laid the note so close to the edge that it almost fell off.

Counselor Denton Briar watched Allie walk past the window and out to meet the rest of her day. He took a sip of his coffee, grinned, and opened the clandestine correspondence.

You're looking mighty fine today, counselor. I may need to see you this Saturday around eight. You know how to find me.

Allie
P.S. Wanda is on to us.

2

The day went by, and the sand in the hourglass traversed the narrow channel of fate a little more carefree than usual. After eating dinner together, Allie and Stan retreated to their nocturnal safe places. For Stan, that meant he was in his room playing Minecraft. Allie was in her favorite chair, but instead of transferring today's writings from her journal to the laptop, she stared at Mr. Morton's number. The light from the phone illuminated her face, highlighting her features like a focused spotlight on a solitary actor on an empty stage. Her mind raced with every reason she shouldn't call, but her inner voice cried, "Hit the call button." So, she did.

On the third ring, a familiar voice answered, "Hello."

"Mr. Morton?"

"This is he?"

"This is Allie McDermitt. We spoke before school today?"

"Allie, I am so glad you called. I have thought about this conversation all day. You mentioned coffee. When would be a good time for you?"

"I am free on Sunday afternoon."

"That's fine. Instead of coffee, how about you and Stan come out to my place? I'll cook lunch."

"That sounds nice, Mr. Morton. Stan is at my mom's this weekend, so it will just be me if that's all right?"

"Well, you know, people in this town talk. I don't want to give the Esthers of Appledale the ammunition to tarnish your reputation."

Allie giggled. "Well, Mr. Morton, I'm a grown unmarried woman, and you are a grown unmarried man. I couldn't care less what people say or think."

"Point taken. Lunch will be ready at two."

"Can I bring anything?"

"Yourself and anything you want to talk about."

"Do you have a wine preference?"

"Not really. Bring what you like, and I'll love it."

"All right. I can do that. Can I ask you another question?"

"Absolutely, Allie. Ask me anything."

"What size shoes do you wear?"

"Excuse me?"

"Just humor me. What size are your shoes?"

Lee Morton sat back in his leather armchair, shook his head, noticed his brown shoes, and chuckled. "Allie, you are as discerning as I remember. Please don't bother yourself with buying me new shoes. I have lots of shoes."

"Mr. Morton, I would like to buy you a new pair of shoes. Will you let me do that for you?"

"I will not. Like I said, I do not need another pair of shoes."

"I'm sorry. I just noticed your shoes today and wanted to do something nice for you. You've done so much for so many." Allie added, "I just wanted to…"

"Don't apologize. There is no need for that. It is the most insightful and thoughtful gesture I have received in ages. I am curious, though. Are you still writing?"

"I have off and on over the years, but I just can't seem to get to the end of the story."

"Does there have to be?"

"Have to be what?"

"An end to a story? Where is the rule that says a story has to end?"

"I don't guess there is a rule for that, is there?"

"No, ma'am. I am pretty sure there isn't. If you get to a point where you need another pair of eyes on your story, I'd be happy to read it."

"I'll keep that in mind, Mr. Morton."

Allie's mind raced. *What if I haven't grown into his expectations of me? What if he hates it? What if he. . .?*

"Allie, no one can judge another's artistic endeavor. We do not critique. We simply ask the two questions I taught you a long time ago. Which were?"

"What is the story, and are you telling it effectively? I can't believe I still remember that."

"The story is there; get out of the way and tell it. What a reader thinks is of no importance. Being true to the story is what matters."

"Not all of this story is fiction."

Mr. Morton stated, “Every fiction is based upon truth. That’s why we believe it. I’m a lot like you, Allie. I have stories only my eyes have seen.”

“We have to be vulnerable.”

“Exactly.”

Allie sat back, stared at her journal, and admitted, “I guess it’s time for both of us to tell our stories.”

“I know I can trust you with my story, and I hope you know you can trust me.”

“I trust you completely, Mr. Morton.”

“These old shoes tell quite a story.” The old man relaxed deep into the plush leather chair. “You can read their tale, and I’ll read whatever story you want to share.”

Silence followed, raging like a stormy sea in an old oil painting; its roar was evident without emitting a decibel.

“Allie? You still there?”

“Yes, I’m still here.”

“Are we in agreement?”

“Can I think about it?”

"Of course you can. I'll know you've accepted my proposal if you arrive Sunday with a manuscript."

"And if I arrive carrying only a bottle of wine?"

"We'll visit, catch up, and discuss whatever topic fate leads us toward."

"OK, Mr. Morton. I'll think about it."

"I'd expect nothing less."

"So, we're all set. Sunday? Two o'clock?"

"Sunday. Two o'clock."

"Goodnight, Mr. Morton."

"Allie, you were born to write. From the first descriptive paragraph you wrote in the seventh grade, I knew there was a story in you. A story only fate can tell."

"Fate's story isn't always easy to read."

"That, my dear scholar, is the truth. I look forward to seeing you on Sunday."

"Me as well."

"Goodnight, Allie."

"Goodnight, Mr. Morton."

They both hung up.

Mr. Morton blew the dust off his composition notebook and retrieved his tarnished silver pencil from his shirt's left breast pocket, leaving the matching fountain pen alone.

Allie opened her laptop and put on her reading glasses.

They both began to write.

The sand in the hourglass traveled to the lower orb where memory and past reside, waiting for the timekeeper to initiate the journey back to the present. The two writers' fevered creativity transported them into a space where time stood still, lost in the story in a way only writers understand. Their tales flowed from their frontal lobes into the codex of language, transferring vision, memory, sense, and smell into encrypted syntax that re-creates alternate universes from black ink and blank space. When viewed through the lens of each imaginer, the sum of experienced realities is limited only by the number of imaginations exposed to that data.

The sun was three hours from bursting forth on the vast, empty horizon of the central Texas sky. Allie shut her laptop, and Mr. Morton put his pencil back in his shirt pocket. Both writers felt the weariness that comes with putting the mind to good use. The teacher and the student fell asleep in their chairs. The sand in the hourglass sat still, but the gears of fate kept turning.

To be continued…

Part Two

1

"Thank you for taking the time to meet with me today."

"Of course, Ms. Shea. I'm Allie McDermitt. It's a pleasure to meet you in person."

Allie sat across from the Appledale Junior High School guidance counselor, who wore navy slacks, a tasteful blouse with sleeves that ended just below the elbow, and red-framed glasses.

"It is nice to meet you as well." The counselor closed her laptop, and the forbidden fruit lost its luminescence. Ms. Shea selected a pen from a polished nickel cylinder that held an even dozen identical pens of the same color. Then she opened a folder labeled "Stanley McDermitt" and asked, "Do you always work this late, Mrs. McDermitt?"

"I work when I'm needed, which can mean late or early."

Ms. Shea referenced a document she'd removed from the labeled folder and asked, "Who looks after Stanley when you work late or early?"

The delicate skin beneath Allie's almond eyes flushed with color. Allie placed her hands in her lap, sat up straight in the chair, and raised her eyes to meet the counselor's gaze. "Stan is thirteen and more than capable of looking after himself while I am five minutes away."

"The issue is not Stan's ability to babysit himself. Studies show that teenagers, boys in particular, from single-parent households have a higher probability of juvenile delinquency and begin to experiment with drugs and alcohol at much higher rates than students who live in a traditional two-parent home. Are you aware of Stan experimenting with drugs, Mrs. McDermitt?"

"Are you?" Allie asked, her face turning as red as her hair.

"No, ma'am. We do not have any data to suggest that."

Allie's hands and arms flew up, creating an enormous W across her torso.

"Then why would you ask me that?"

"Students who lack parental supervision often become susceptible to drug and alcohol use. So, can you tell me who watches Stanley when you are working early or late?"

Allie's eyes leaped across the desk. She clasped her hands together, strangling the thin air, wishing the space between her clenched fingers was Ms. Shea's perfect little neck. The lines on her forehead creased, and Allie, in a soft voice, fired back, "Ms. Shea, Stan has an excellent academic record, shows no signs of experimenting with drugs, and hasn't even shown an interest in girls yet. Whether or not Stan is supervised or unsupervised for whatever length of time I deem appropriate is none of your business. Why am I here?"

Ms. Shea set the document on top of the file folder and arranged the edges to ensure parallel alignment, unaware that the soft voice was the one she should fear. "Allie—may I call you Allie?"

"My friends call me Allie. Until you are one of those, I prefer Mrs. McDermitt."

"I see." Ms. Shea cleared her throat. "Of course, Mrs. McDermitt. As a school, we are working diligently to engage in interventions to identify and provide resources to students and families we have identified to be at risk."

"At risk of what?"

"At risk of not graduating from high school."

"He's in the seventh grade. Aren't you getting a little ahead of yourself?"

"This school and the state of Texas don't think so."

"Wait a minute." Allie blinked and rubbed her temples. Then she placed her hands back on her thighs with an audible slap and asked, "Why do you and the great state of Texas think Stan is at risk?"

Ms. Shea glanced down and referenced the document. "We use multiple factors to determine whether a child is at risk. Stan is an average student academically; his teachers have all given positive feedback concerning his behavior, interactions with friends and classmates, and his participation in classroom activities. However, being an only child of a single parent who lost his father at such a young age puts him at risk of not completing high school. Socioeconomic status may also be a factor, but I couldn't get definitive data to confirm that. Why hasn't Stan returned his free and reduced lunch program form?"

"Free and reduced lunch form?"

"Yes, ma'am. The application was in his enrollment paperwork, but Stan did not return it on the first day of school. Mrs. McDermitt, there is nothing stigmatizing about applying for free and reduced lunches."

"Stigmatizing?"

"I'm sorry. 'Stigmatizing' means…"

"Ms. Shea, I know what stigmatizing means. Don't talk down to me."

Ms. Shea cleared her throat. "Mrs. McDermitt, this is not a handout. It is a hand up."

Allie's face glowed crimson, and she unsuccessfully took a deep breath to calm herself. "Hand up? Ms. Shea, do you have children?"

"No."

"How long have you been teaching?"

"I taught in the classroom for two years, and this is my first year as a counselor."

"So, you are going to sit there and tell me, a woman who is raising her son on her own, that her kid is at risk. You've been a teacher for three years and think you know how to parent my kid better than I do. I've been a parent longer than you have been licensed to drive."

"Mrs. McDermitt, I think we got off on the wrong foot here."

"Really? What gave you that idea?"

"The purpose of this meeting is to give you the resources you need to make sure your son completes his academic journey. I am here to let you know that you are not alone. We have resources and activities that can help you and Stan."

"What kind of help do you think I need?"

"For starters, free or reduced lunch could lessen the financial burden on you, and studies show students who are food secure are more likely to be successful academically."

"Are you serious? Food insecure? The boy never stops eating."

"That's exactly why free lunches can help lessen your financial burden."

Allie's hands leaped from her lap; she crossed her arms across her chest and sat back in the chair. "OK, Ms. Shea. How much do I have to make to qualify for this hand up?"

Ms. Shea removed another document from the folder. "A family with one child whose income is less than $26,800 per year, but families making up to $37,000 per year can receive meals at a reduced rate."

Allie's face grew tense; every facial feature that could wrinkle creased. "All I have to do is fill out that form and give you my personal financial information, and somehow, my son will no longer be at risk?"

"No, Stan will always be considered at risk."

"I assure you, I make double the starting teacher salary in this town. My income is not an issue. What do you need to take my son off this at-risk list?"

"If your financial health is confirmed, Stan could be removed from the list if you remarried."

"Oh, my goodness, sweetheart. Did anyone ever train you in the most effective ways to piss off a mom?" The counselor looked down at her desk. "No? Well, you're really good at it."

"Mrs. McDermitt."

"Let's start with this little tidbit. I will not give you my financial information other than to say my income is much more than $37,000. I do not need nor do I qualify for free or reduced lunch. There isn't a stigma to be stigmatized by, Ms. Shea. I do not qualify. That is why I never returned the form."

"Uhm, Mrs...."

Allie held out her hand with her palm facing Ms. Shea and scoffed, "Oh, sweetheart, I'm not finished. You began this conversation by asking questions that insulted me as a mother and as a woman."

"That wasn't my..."

Allie extended her palm, and Ms. Shea got the message.

Allie placed her hands back on her lap and added, "This is a small town, and being a woman here is hard. You'll learn that firsthand if you start your other meetings like you started this one. I'm a single mother, a widow of a local boy who came back from the desert a shell of the man who left, and I am doing my very best to raise my boy to become a man. Then some idealistic little g..."

Allie closed her eyes and took a slow, deep brcath. "A young woman who taught for two years before getting a counselor job implies that I don't properly supervise or feed my kid. If that weren't enough, you tell me the only way my kid is going to be off the 'at-risk' list is for me to remarry, as if a man is the only solution for every problem a woman can have. Did you learn about women's suffrage and rights in college, or were you asleep in the sorority house during that lecture?"

"Mrs. McDermitt, I am only trying to help and give you resources to help Stan be successful. I did not mean to offend you. I cannot imagine how hard it must be to raise a son on your own. That is why I called this meeting."

"Ms. Shea, play this back in your overeducated mind and see if any of your actions or statements met any of the intentions you set for this meeting. Whether it was a lack of experience, stupidity, or the combination of both, you failed to do any of those things you just said. None of them."

"Mrs. McDermitt, I am so sorry."

Allie blew a stray hair from her face and retorted, “You’re lucky, Ms. Shea. You still live in a world where you believe you can fix everything, overcome every hardship, and heal every broken life. The older you get and the more life you experience, you will see you have no control over any of it. Fate wrote the story well before you or I had the chance to read it, and we don’t have editing privileges. You can’t fix everything with a program. You can’t. I can’t. Stan can’t. We do the best we can and pray to God that fate wrote a happy ending for us.”

“I can see why you feel that way about life. I cannot imagine losing a husband. I haven’t even found one yet.”

Allie’s wrinkles relaxed, and a smile stretched across her tired face. “Just be glad this happened with me instead of some of the other parents in this town. They’d be banging down the principal’s door before you could explain yourself. Have you talked with Stan about this?”

“This evaluation was made by analyzing the data. I haven’t actually met Stan yet.”

Allie stood and shook her head. “Kiddo, before you ever label a kid anything and decide to share that label with the kid's mother, meet the kid first. This meeting is over."

Allie looked Ms. Shea squarely in the eyes. "What happened tonight will stay here and between us."

"I appreciate that."

"But be warned, Ms. Shea. If Stan ever comes home and tells me he is labeled as or treated like an 'at-risk' kid, I will take a lot more than your job."

The young lady swallowed, and her eyes sank as she focused on placing the documents parallel with the folder.

"Do I make myself clear, Ms. Shea?"

Ms. Shea's voice quivered, and a tear rolled down her cheek. "Yes, ma'am, Mrs. McDermitt. I am so sorry."

In that moment, Allie knew she had to attempt to salvage this disaster of a meeting. She collected herself and acknowledged, "I know you asked me here with the best of intentions. I recognize that. Being a parent isn't something you learn in college, and the best way to reach a kid can't be found in statistics and forms."

"I have so much to learn."

"Yes, sweetheart. You do. What is your first name, Ms. Shea?"

"It's Tessa."

"Tessa, your heart is in the right place. You want to help kids. I get that. Other parents in this town will not. Learn to tread lightly and don't meet with a parent until you've talked to the kid."

Another tear rolled down Ms. Shea's cheek, and Allie reached for the tissues sitting on the filing cabinet to the left of the desk.

"One more thing. Don't ever let them see you cry. They'll take it as weakness." Allie handed Ms. Shea the tissues. "When you show weakness, the wolves will strike. Women like us have to be strong, even when we're not."

Allie reached across the desk and placed her hand on the young counselor's quivering hands. Tessa Shea set her glasses on the desk and dabbed the tears away from under her eyes like a beauty consultant applying blush.

Tessa collected herself, put her glasses back on, and said, "Thank you."

Allie patted the back of her hand. "You're welcome, Tessa, and you can call me Allie."

Ms. Shea looked up. "Thank you, Allie."

“Have a good night, and thanks again for meeting so late.”

“You’re welcome.”

“Do yourself a favor. Meet Stanley. You’ll see what all that data can’t. The only thing that kid is at risk of is growing up too soon and breaking his momma’s heart.”

Allie left the school and walked to her car. Tessa Shea began making calls and rescheduling parent conferences.

2

The days between that meeting at dusk and Saturday evening were uneventful, like life can be. Routines, daily chores, and life's little monotonies carried Allie to the weekend and her clandestine rendezvous with a certain handsome lawyer.

Denton Briar looked out the window into the backyard in an old bathrobe and nursed a nightcap of neat scotch. The sun sank into the western horizon. Apple and tangerine hues sprayed across the plains in a useless attempt to hang on to the day just a little longer.

Allie came into the kitchen wearing Denton's button-down shirt and declared, "Counselor, I'm afraid this judge intends to hold you in contempt."

"Again? Really?"

"The punishment must fit the crime."

"What crime am I committing, Mrs. McDermitt?"

"You're prying open my heart, good sir."

"Your Honor is doing the same."

Allie smiled and reached for her stemless wine glass. The burgundy liquid ran down the crystal, leaving veins, and it smelled of sweet oak with a hint of blackberry. She took a sip and asked, "Can we promise not to say it?"

"Not say what?"

"You know, the words you can't take back."

"Oh, those words." He looked down and took another sip of his golden liquid, which had turned cloudy as the ice and scotch mingled.

"Allie, I'm not ready for that either, but that doesn't mean I don't feel them." The dapper lawyer walked up behind the justice, placed his arms around her waist, laid his head on her shoulder, gently kissed her neck just below the left ear, and whispered, "I'll tell you this. I know if I did say it, I'd mean it."

"I would, too." She turned around, clasped his face in her hands, and gave him a little peck on the tip of his nose. "That's why we shouldn't say it. Not yet, anyway."

The prisoner looked up at the clock above the kitchen sink. “Do I have to leave, or can I stay the night?”

“Counselor, you are held in contempt until six a.m. tomorrow morning. At which time, you will be released on bond.”

“And what, may I ask, is the collateral securing this bond?”

“Your heart.”

Before the sun awoke from its slumber and illuminated the cotton gin and grain silos that dotted the edge of Appledale, Allie watched from her living room as her Saturday night prisoner drove away, his headlights cutting the darkness before his worn pickup.

“Allison Briar,” she spoke into the empty room. “I could get used to that.”

Allie opened her laptop, slipped on her reading glasses, and got to work.

3

At a quarter of two that afternoon, Allie walked up the steps of an old farmhouse that took cover from the wind within an open box of thick cedars. The conifer windbreak opened to the east. An easterly wind in this part of the world was as unlikely as meeting a Democrat. The heavy oak door stood open, but a screen door protected the interior from flies and mosquitoes. She placed the manuscript under her arm that held a bottle of wine, and pressed the doorbell. She heard Mr. Morton's voice from inside.

"Allie, come on in. I'm in the kitchen."

She walked through the front room, and the aroma of something extraordinary made her realize how hungry she was. She hadn't had anything other than coffee since she released Denton from his overnight sentence.

"That smells amazing. What is it?"

The kitchen counter sat under a thin film of flour, the handle of a dough-spattered rolling pin pointed up from the sink, and an assortment of fish, shrimp, and scallops waited on the end-grain cutting board for their trip to the sauté pan. Thin lengths of angel hair pasta hung over a wooden rack, waiting to plunge into the pot of boiling water that spewed forth steam on the back burner of the range.

"I don't have guests very often. I hope I still remember how to cook this."

"It smells like you remember. Did you make that pasta from scratch?"

"Oh, yes. That and the sauce. You want a taste?"

"Yes, I do."

Mr. Morton handed Allie a spoon, and she dipped it into the saucepan, raised it to her nose, and sniffed. When she placed the spoon in her mouth, her eyebrows raised, and her face lit up with surprise. Emphasizing each syllable, she professed, "That is amazing."

"Thank you. It's a recipe I learned a long time ago. In a different world, really."

Allie set the bottle of wine and her manuscript on the table. "I decided to bring you the first few chapters of my unfinished novel."

Mr. Morton wiped his hands on the crisply starched white apron that protected his faded blue jeans and long-sleeved Oxford shirt, walked into the living room, and picked up his composition notebook. "This hasn't been out of my living room since the day I moved in." He handed it over to her and admitted, "I could use a glass of that wine, Allie."

"Me, too."

Mr. Morton took the corkscrew from the kitchen drawer, passed it to Allie, grabbed two wine glasses from the cupboard, and returned to cooking. Allie removed the cork, poured the wine, and set a glass on the counter beside the stove within reach of Mr. Morton. He took a sip.

"Oh my. That is good."

"Yes, it is."

“I’ve set the table out in the garden for lunch. Why don’t you go out there, make yourself comfortable, and give that a read?” He pointed to his notebook on the table.

“You don’t need any help in here?”

“No, ma’am. Lunch will be done in about fifteen minutes. The day is too pretty to spend in this old house. I’ll be out in a minute.”

Allie walked through the back screened door with her wine in one hand and Mr. Morton’s writing in the other. To call the Eden Mr. Morton had created out of the dusty farmland a garden would be as inept as calling New York City a hamlet. It was breathtaking. A teak table and four chairs sat on a flagstone patio shaded from the sun by a trellis covered in climbing roses. Lush grass spread from the patio in an oval surrounded by cascading layers of wildflowers broken only by the rock path that led back to the tin-roofed farmhouse. The gentle breeze that blew through the cedar windbreak carried a blend of evergreen and fully blossomed sage’s sweet perfume, which all Texans sing about and then clap four times. A dog as black as onyx with sprinkles of white on her muzzle, the tips of her paws, and her long, floppy ears looked up at Allie as she approached. Sensing no threat, the dog returned to her dream, where she had strong legs, and squirrels weren't so fast.

Allie sat under the shade of the roses, set down her wine glass, pulled her reading glasses out of her pocketbook and put them on, opened the notebook, and began to read. The sands of time poured into the globe of the past. With every word, Allie began to understand the old brown shoes. More importantly, she began to understand the man, Lee Morton. The journal wasn't filled with fiction. Each entry was dated and signed; the first date was December 2, 1978. The handwriting was impeccable. Errors were crossed out with a single line, just as he taught her. It was Mr. Morton's diary.

Mr. Morton set the feast before his guest and insisted, "Don't want this to get cold."

Allie wiped a tear with a folded napkin from the table and looked up. "Mr. Morton, I had no idea."

"No one does, Allie. No one has ever read that, and anyone who knew or could have known is either dead or was never born."

"I don't understand."

“Neither do I. Let’s eat. We can talk after. I see Lacy didn’t bother you.”

“Nope. She took one look at me and went right back to sleep.”

They ate their fill and drank their wine as the shade crept, inch by inch, over the lawn. Without a word, each author picked up the other’s writing and read. Time marched on. *Tick, tock.* Shade began its domination over the light that had filled the garden. The past roared off every page, colliding with the present, asking questions they both knew would never be answered in this life.

Allie set Mr. Morton’s notebook beside her dinner plate, sipped her wine, and watched as two robins danced back and forth from the sage bushes to their nest on the leeward side of the cedars. The old dog half barked in her sleep, her legs trotting out in a quick gait, propelling her back into her youth. Like the dog, Allie and Mr. Morton could not avoid the present or the future. Neither could they ignore nor forget their past. Fate laid the tracks of their lives before either engine traveled the path to this moment, where their tracks merged into the present. Each train received a new boxcar to stow away and carry the memories from this present back from the past and forward into their futures. Over time, the train grows longer, adding new boxcars to fill with the cargo that was, is, and will be their life. No matter the length of the train, the view from the caboose holds steadfast and unchanging. The past recedes into the distance, slipping farther away, details grow vague, and the future creeps closer, but its course never changes.

Allie looked up and saw Mr. Morton had finished reading. They both had. They gathered their dinner dishes without a word, walked into the kitchen, and placed them in the sink.

Allie began loading the dirty dishes into the dishwasher, and Mr. Morton wiped down the stove and the countertops. The residue from the exquisite meal washed down the drain and into memory. Allie walked back into the living room and noticed the bookcase and the mantel for the first time. The old leather glove had a price tag still attached. She turned around and saw Mr. Morton standing next to his chair.

"She was pregnant when she died?"

"Observant as always, Mrs. McDermitt."

"Did you know it was a boy?"

“No, but her dad was hopeful.” Mr. Morton put his hands in his pockets and looked down at the floor.

Allie looked at the books filling every inch of the bookcases. “Fate writes a tale that’s hard to read.”

“And even harder to write.”

Allie shook her head and looked at the glove. “Fate is a bitch.”

“She most certainly is, my bright scholar. She certainly is.”

Allie stepped toward Mr. Morton, wrapped her arms around him, and declared, “Today was magnificent.”

He hugged her back. “It certainly has been.”

“Can we do this again next Sunday?”

They parted. “I don’t see why not.”

“Let’s take a week, digest these stories, make notes and suggestions, and have lunch at my house. Fair warning, I am not as good a cook as you.”

Mr. Morton giggled. “This wasn’t about the food. Was it?”

“No, sir. It was not.”

Mr. Morton scratched the white whiskers on his chin. "Allie, I don't really want you to edit my work."

"But..."

"Allie, listen to me. I am an old man, and that is one of many journals I have kept since I was eight years old." The aged educator pointed to the table beside his easy chair. Its lower shelves were stacked full of notebooks. "That was just a few mournful months of my journey. There are so many more experiences locked inside these journals. I want you to use them as inspiration. You have the liberty of not writing my life in the first person. You can look at this story as a spectator, not a participant. I want you to use your insight and talent to embellish, add to, take away from, and craft from it a novel about an average man and the life he led."

"Mr. Morton, I can't write a story that only you can tell."

"Allie, you are the only one who can. Embellish, edit, and weave together all the fodder into the story you were born to write."

"Are you sure about this?"

"I've never been more sure of anything in my life. You can turn all this into something transcendent. I know it."

Mr. Morton pulled a cardboard box from the closet and stacked the journals inside. Allie held the screen door open, and they walked down the steps to Allie's blue sedan. Allie opened the trunk, and Mr. Morton placed the journals inside.

"One stipulation, Allie."

"What's that, Mr. Morton?"

"Finish your novel first. I will help you with that. But the other one is for your eyes only."

"You aren't going to read it."

"I don't have to."

"Why not?"

"I lived it. I want you to tell it. I do not need to read it."

"What if I want you to?"

"That's a conversation for another day. I trust that everything you read in my journals stays between us. Even after I'm dead, you mustn't tell anyone the source of your book."

"You're serious. Aren't you?"

"Yes, I am."

Allie placed her hands on his shoulders. “Mr. Morton, I will write it to the best of my ability.”

“I’d expect nothing less.”

They embraced and said their goodbyes.

When Stan got home, Allie sat in her chair so engrossed in her work that she didn’t hear him come in. Stan tapped her on the shoulder.

“*Shit*. Stan, you scared me to death.” The notebook fell to the floor.

“Jeez, Mom. Potty mouth.”

“Did you have fun?”

“Yeah. Is there anything to eat?”

“Make yourself a sandwich.”

“OK!” Stan hustled into the kitchen on a mission.

“Your new razor, shaving cream, deodorant, and cologne are in the bag hanging on your bedroom door.”

“Thanks.”

“You’re welcome, Stan the Man.”

“Mom!”

The constellations rose above the bursting cotton bulbs, anticipating the roars of the combines. Front porch lights turned on one by one, and darkness settled over sleepy Appledale. Lacy, the once legendary squirrel chaser, followed Mr. Morton into the bedroom and watched as the old scholar crawled into bed, but the light remained on in the living room of the two-bedroom cottage Allie and Stan called home. And as she would for many months to come, Allie McDermitt fell asleep in her chair.

To be continued...

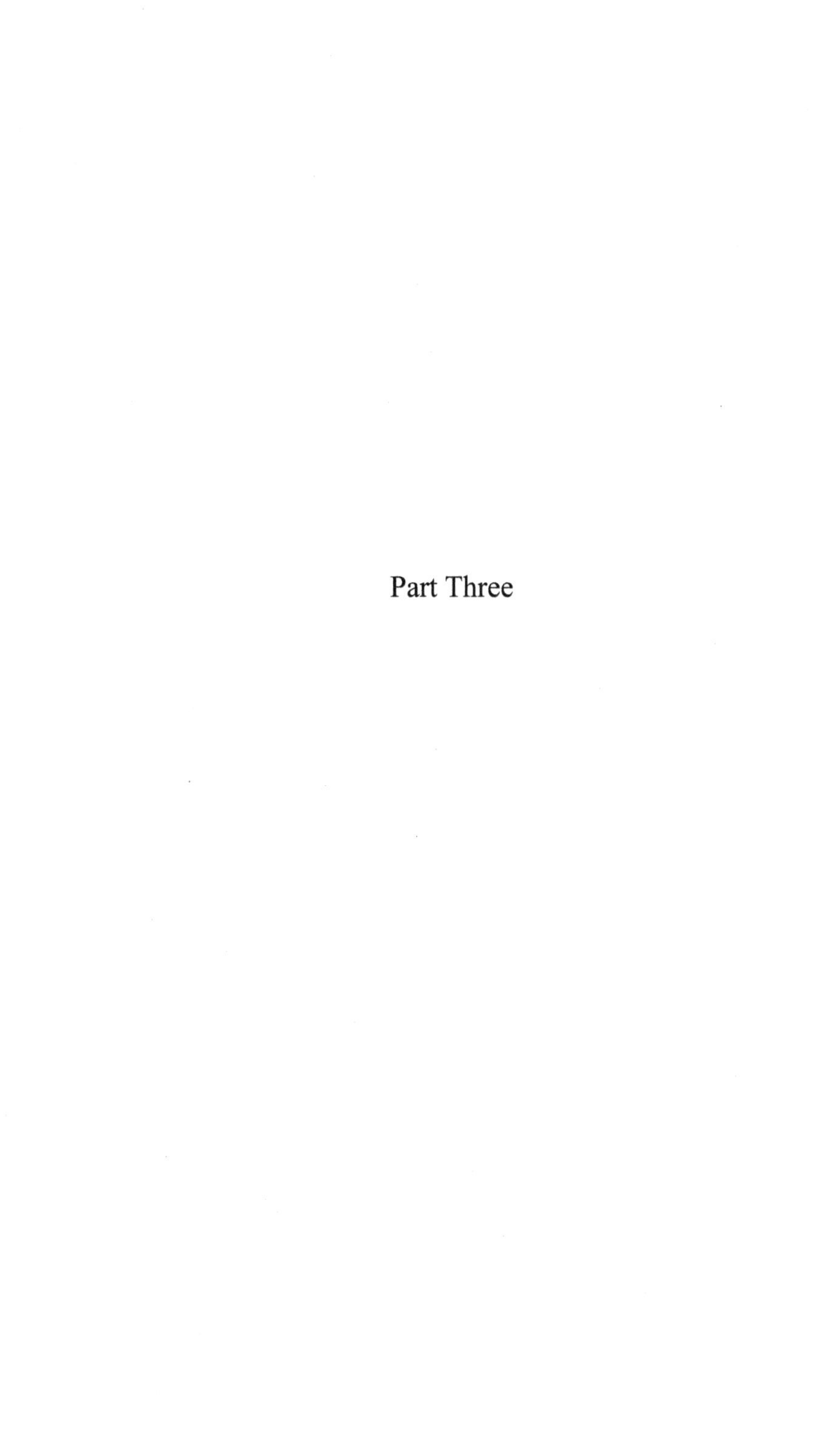

Part Three

1

When she was eight, Alice Henderson briefly held the world record for filling her mouth with marbles. On the Monday following her lunch with Mr. Morton, Alice Henderson, known now as Allie McDermitt, stepped up to the plate and inserted her entire foot into her mouth.

Allie walked up the steps to the entrance of Appledale Junior High School, holding one of those bags that make a gift-wrapping novice appear to be an aficionado. The crimson bag was filled with a bouquet of violet-and-ivory tissue paper, fluffed and stuffed to perfection. Allie stepped to the glass door, pressed the buzzer, and a familiar voice answered.

"May I help you?"

"Yes, Mrs. Shirley. This is Allie McDermitt."

"Allie, you just get yourself on in here."

The remote-controlled lock mechanism clunked, and Allie entered the reception area. Mrs. Shirley approached with outstretched arms and cheered, "Honey, it's so good to see you."

Mrs. Shirley wrapped her arms as far around Allie as they could reach. This wasn't a problem for an average woman because Allie did not have a large circumference, but Mrs. Shirley was just a hint larger than the scary woman who kept saying, "Go to the light" in *Poltergeist*.

The small-statured receptionist released the hug, and Allie replied, "It's good to see you, too."

Mrs. Shirley led Allie to the red bench across from her desk, which students, past and present, called the "hot seat." Allie sat down.

Mrs. Shirley took her seat and shared, "I can't believe how much Stanley looks like Jimmy."

"I know, right?"

"Can't deny that boy is a McDermitt. Not that anyone would want to."

Mrs. Shirley possessed the gift or the curse of not changing with time. She looked exactly as Allie remembered, except her eyes. They were tired.

All too often, Allie observed the wearying effect of widowhood in her own.

A tasteful arrangement of fresh flowers sat in a transparent blue vase at the edge of her desk. A handwritten note was held in place by three forked fingers of a green plastic stem, perfectly placed among the fragrant blooms.

"Ooh, Mrs. Shirley, who's the secret Romeo?"

Mrs. Shirley thumped the card and giggled. "I'm not that lucky! It's secretary's week. I'd prefer a raise. A secret admirer would be even better, but flowers are nice, too. Are you picking up Stanley?"

"No, ma'am. I'd like to see Ms. Shea if she's available."

"Is she expecting you?"

"I don't think so. We had an appointment last week, but things didn't go well."

"Oh, what happened?"

"Let's just say she had the best of intentions but failed miserably despite her best efforts, and my lack of a filter didn't help, either."

"Allie McDermitt has a filter? Better call CNN."

Allie looked down at the crimson peace offering and divulged, “I brought her a little something to make up for it.”

“How sweet of you. You know she’s pretty new at this. Right?”

Allie rolled her eyes. “How does someone with so little experience get a job like that?”

Mrs. Shirley looked up, her weary eyes focused, and retorted, “Did you need ten years of experience the first time you took an X-ray?”

Allie chuckled. “Well, I don’t take X-rays. I do echocardiograms and sonograms.”

“Allie, you know what I meant.”

“I do, but how can a person without kids have any idea what it takes to raise one?”

Mrs. Shirley’s fingers rolled rhythmically, pinky to thumb, like the right hand of a pianist playing a descending scale. She looked down at her desk, then back to Allie and answered, “I never had kids; none of my own, anyway. Hundreds. Thousands of kids have come through these doors. Plus, one niece and two nephews. Not being a mother doesn’t mean I don’t know a thing or two about kids.”

Allie looked down at the floor, desperately hoping to find an escape pod, a trap door, an ejection seat; anything to get herself out of the "hot seat." Her hands sank deep into her pockets for a key to open a speedy exit. Finding none, she looked up. "That's not what I meant."

Mrs. Shirley's fingers ceased their percussive scale; the pitter-patter of fingernails on wood was replaced by "the look." Allie remembered how even the toughest boys in school would shrink a foot when Mrs. Shirley's eyes landed on them. Once again, the tiny woman behind "the look" was not as tiny as she appeared.

"What did you mean, Allie?"

"I just meant that a college degree hanging on a wall and being able to read data in some study doesn't mean you know enough to tell a mom how to parent their kid. That little girl told me the only way Stan could get off her "at-risk " list was for me to remarry. Can you believe that?"

"Really? That little girl said that? Hmm. Well? Would that be such a bad thing?"

Allie crossed her arms and huffed. "Seriously? You, too?"

"I'm sorry. None of my business."

"Correct, and it's none of Ms. Shea's, either. Why are you being so defensive about her, anyway?"

Mrs. Shirley looked down at the phone, pressed the speaker button, entered an extension, and the phone began to ring. After the second ring, the counselor replied, "This is Ms. Shea."

"Good morning, Tessa."

Ms. Shea's voice returned over the speaker. "Hey, Aunt Rhonda. What's up?"

Mrs. Shirley's tired eyes looked up, her nose scrunched, and her left eyebrow rose in silent response to Allie's *Why are you being so defensive about her, anyway?*

"Mrs. McDermitt is here and would like to see you. Are you available?"

Ms. Shea responded, "I'll be right down."

Mrs. Shirley pressed the button and ended the call. The two women glared at each other. Mrs. Shirley broke first, glanced back down at her hand, and resumed practicing the pentatonic pattern. Allie looked into the blue vase of flowers, and in its reflection, saw her eight-year-old self with a mouth full of marbles, whispering, "A foot fits, too."

Mrs. Shirley reached across the desk and took Allie's hand. "Oh, honey, we're all defensive about our own blood. It's only natural."

"Yeah, I guess it is."

"She'll always be a little girl to me. You're not the first momma who had shoe leather for breakfast this morning."

"Rough day?"

"At least you didn't call the principal. The others did."

"I hate that."

Mrs. Shirley gave Allie "the look" and emphasized, "She likes to learn the hard way. Like someone else I know."

"I hope she grows out of it. Lord knows I haven't."

"Not many of us do. Cough it up to being human."

Allie sat in the "hot seat" like a little girl with a mouthful of marbles, chewing on the stringy remains of a jumbo slice of humble pie, and unconsciously rubbed her wedding band. She drifted into her dreamland of solitude, alone with the characters in her stories who, with a single line, could effortlessly transform an awkward self-inflicted conflict into an ideal resolution. But Allie wasn't a character in one of her stories; she withdrew and left the perfect dialogue to the gnomes of her imagination.

"Mrs. McDermitt?" Ms. Shea asked with no response. "Allie?"

Allie heard her voice, but it was like holding a shell up to your left ear, hearing the roar of the sea, and attempting to focus in on a conversation across a crowded restaurant with your right.

Mrs. Shirley and Ms. Shea looked at their visitor, who seemed lost in thought, and shrugged.

Ms. Shea touched her shoulder and asked, "Allie, are you OK?"

Allie stirred, closed her imagination's notebook, and answered, "Yes. Perfectly fine. Thank you."

Allie stood, shook Tessa's hand, and asked, "Do you have a few minutes?"

"Of course."

Allie glanced toward the blue vase, hoping to glean some advice from her eight-year-old self, but her apparition had found the secret escape route, leaving Allie to suffer this treatise alone.

They walked past Mrs. Shirley's desk and down the hallway toward Ms. Shea's office.

Mrs. Shirley advised, "You girls behave, now."

Allie and Tessa chorused, "Yes, ma'am."

Ms. Shea led Allie down the hallway and into her office, shutting the door behind them.

Allie announced, "I brought you something," placed the red bag on the tidy desktop, and took a seat.

Tessa sat across from Allie. "That is so sweet, Allie. Thank you."

"When I saw it, I knew it was meant for you."

Tessa removed the tissue paper and saw a translucent glass orb, perfectly symmetrical except for the flat underside. She pulled it from the bag, looked at it in the light, and announced, "It's a paperweight."

"Take a closer look."

Tessa picked up the paperweight, held it in front of the reading light, which was mounted to the desk with an adjustable arm, and blurted, "Oh, my goodness. What's in there? It's microscopic."

"A mustard seed."

"A mustard seed? Like the parable?"

"Exactly. Most people miss the message of that parable. Faith is important, but the impact a purposely planted seed can have is truly limitless. That little speck is a reminder that it only takes a seed to change a shapeless void into a blossoming plant."

Tessa leaned into her headrest and affirmed, "That makes more sense than moving mountains."

"Unless you own Caterpillar stock and a significant amount of dynamite, that mountain's not going anywhere."

Tessa smiled and replied, "I love it. Thank you."

"You're welcome. We all have days when we feel like giving up. When you do, remember that you matter. Use it as a reminder that, like the tiny mustard seed, you can make a difference."

Tessa carefully placed the talisman of encouragement next to a bright pink day planner and remarked, "That is so thoughtful. I see where Stanley gets it from."

"So, you met Stan?"

"Yes, I did, and he is very bright, Allie. Very insightful. I see it's genetic."

"He's a lot more insightful than I was at his age."

"He's such a sweet young man. By the way, you were right. The only thing Stan is at risk of is growing up and breaking his momma's heart."

Allie agreed. "Growing up way too fast. I bought him his first razor and deodorant this weekend, and he's been using the last of his dad's cologne."

"Puberty can be a challenge."

"Yes, it can."

"He certainly has taken a liking to Mr. Morton."

Allie smiled. "I was in his class the year I moved here. That's where I first met my husband."

Ms. Shea cleared her throat. "Mr. Morton shared something Stan wrote in his class."

"Really?"

"Mr. Morton asked them to…"

"Write their first memory," interrupted Allie, finishing Tessa's sentence.

"How'd you know that?"

"Everyone who takes Mr. Morton's class never forgets that assignment."

Tessa inhaled, looked at Allie, and said, "I'd like you to read it."

She slid a white sealed envelope across the desk and explained, "I made you a copy. Don't read it here. It's personal, and you'll want to take some time to process this."

Allie crossed her arms, shook her head, and inquired, "What does that mean?"

"Trust me, it's not a bad thing. It's quite beautiful. For a seventh grader, Stan has a way with words. I wonder where he gets that from?"

"Mr. Morton is a great teacher."

"Stan didn't learn this in a week, Allie. This is a gift."

"You think so?"

"I know so. Can I share something with you about gifts?"

"Of course, Tessa."

"When I was a kid, I loved to sing. I sang everywhere. My voice put me through college."

"I had no idea."

"How could you?"

Tessa explained, "In the middle of my junior year of college, my father died of cancer."

"I'm so sorry."

"In the end, he was ready. Dad died on Christmas Day. That night, my mother told me he wanted me to sing at his service. I was mortified." Tessa shook her head and fumed. "No! I was angry! Part of me wanted to do it, but I didn't think I could. How could I be expected to sing my Dad's favorite hymn when I couldn't keep my shit, sorry, stuff together."

"No, 'shit' is definitely appropriate. I know all too well how grief works, unfortunately."

"I know you do. I met with our pastor and told him I couldn't do it. We sat on the pew where my mom and dad sat every Sunday I could remember, and he told me something that changed my life. He explained, 'God doesn't let us choose our gifts and talents, but when given the opportunity, we're expected to use them.'"

"Tessa, that's a lot of pressure."

"It is, but I gained something else from that advice. Have you ever seen God at work?"

"All the time."

"No, I mean physically, God in the flesh, on the earth, working to improve our lives or answer our prayers."

Allie shook her head. “No, I don’t guess I have.”

“So, how do you know it was God’s work?”

Allie sat back in the chair, her eyebrows tensed, and she looked up. “God works through us. We are his hands and feet.”

“Exactly. What would happen if we chose not to act? Not to use our gifts?”

Allie’s brows relaxed, her eyes focused on the tiny speck held inside the glass orb, and she delineated, “People won’t see God or, more importantly, they won’t experience his love.”

“My pastor told me that God gave me this voice and the choice to use it was mine and mine alone.”

Allie leaned forward and asked, “So, what did you do?”

“I went into full performance mode, lost myself in the character of the song, and did what I was trained to do. I stayed in character to the very last note. Then, I sat in the pew next to my mom and Aunt Rhonda and melted.”

“You were like the mustard seed.”

“Yeah, I guess I was. But, you know, you’re pretty remarkable, too.”

Allie shrugged. "I don't know about that."

"Well, I do. Mr. Morton does, too. I think everyone in town knows how special you are."

Allie shook her head and confided, "I don't see it."

"I never saw it in me, either. No one likes the sound of their own voice. Especially a singer."

"A singer who doesn't like the sound of their own voice? That's strange."

"It's true. As a singer, you have to trust someone else to mold and shape your voice because what you hear is never what everyone else does."

"I guess that makes sense. I hate listening to my voice mail greeting. Doesn't sound like me at all."

"I know. Right? I don't hear myself sing the way others can, and you don't see yourself the way others do, Allie. You can't see it, but believe me, you're a remarkable woman."

"I don't know what to say."

"You don't have to say anything. Stan is remarkable, too, just like his mother. Listen, you don't have to read that today or even tomorrow. But, when the time is right, and you are ready, you need to read it."

Tessa reached for a tissue, used it to dry her running mascara, and sighed. “Allie, it’s beautiful.”

“Are you sure Stan wants me to read it?”

Tessa shook her head. “I asked him. He told me, ‘I wrote this for my mom.’”

Allie had no mascara to worry about, but whispered, “I’m going to need one of those.”

Tessa peeled another tissue from the box and handed it to Allie. “I’m pretty sure a writer feels the same way about their writing as a singer does about their voice.”

“Did Mr. Morton put you up to this?”

“He just mentioned you are a phenomenal writer. Do you still write?”

“I do.”

Tessa placed her clasped hands on the desk and explained, “An editor can help shape your writing the same way a voice teacher helps a singer find their pure voice. The hardest part about singing is getting out of the way and letting the sound out.”

“Mr. Morton always says, ‘Get out of the way and tell the story.’ Makes sense, I guess.”

"Can we meet for lunch? Sometimes, I need to get out of this building during the day."

"I would love to. You have my number?"

"Yes, I do. Thank you again. The gift means more than I can say."

"You're welcome."

Ms. Shea walked Mrs. McDermitt back to the front desk.

"You girls bury the hatchet back there, or do I need to call the SRO?" asked Mrs. Shirley.

Allie and Tessa looked at Aunt Rhonda and smiled. "We're good."

Allie waved. "Goodbye, Mrs. Shirley."

"Great to see you again, Allie. We will keep an eye on Stan for you."

"I appreciate that."

Allie made her way to the parking lot holding Stan's envelope. From the car, she called the hospital's receptionist, held the phone to her ear, looked at the envelope resting on the passenger seat, and asked, "Linda, do I have anything scheduled this afternoon?"

Allie breathed a sigh of relief. "OK. I'll have my cell phone. Call if anything changes. Thank you, Linda."

The engine of Allie's car came to life, and she drove to the end of the parking lot, activated the turn signal, and pointed the car toward the city limit sign.

2

The slight rise on the Texas plain north of Appledale had a population two times that of the small community. Everyone on this hill was from Appledale or had at least died here. Row upon row of granite and marble markers lay aligned, facing east, waiting for a trumpet to play and call them home. Some graves were marked with great fanfare; others still held the tin sign with copper letters that slid in and out like the price-per-gallon sign at Allsup's. People either forgot or couldn't afford the large stone emblems.

Allie parked her car, got out, and walked among the quiet residents to a place she usually only visited once a year. The grave marker was simple, like many in cemeteries across America, and was given to veterans at no cost. Most lay at the foot of a grave in the shadow of a more prominent memorial, but James C. McDermitt's marker was placed at the head.

Allie sat cross-legged, dusted the dirt and leaves off the gravestone, and said, "It's been a minute. I still think about you every day.

"Stan started seventh grade last week, and guess what? He's in Mr. Morton's class. Do you remember the assignment we had the first week of school, the one about our first memory? Stan got the same one. It's a long story, but that's why I'm here.

"You would have laughed at me today. The new school counselor and I didn't exactly get off on the right foot, but do you remember little Mrs. Shirley? Well, I was telling Mrs. Shirley all the reasons why Ms. Shea, uhm Tessa, wasn't qualified to give me advice about parenting, etc., you know, being myself. Well, guess what? She's Mrs. Shirley's niece."

Allie looked up, and a gentle breeze rustled the grass beside her.

"Anyway, I had bought Ms. Shea, Tessa, a gift to make up for our horrible first meeting. It wasn't all my fault, but I didn't really help it, either. While I was there, Tessa gave me Stan's assignment. Tessa said it was for me. He wanted me to read it. It's here in this envelope."

Allie wiped a tear from her cheek. "That's why I'm here. I want you to hear it, too. But first, I have to tell you something. It might be hard to hear because it's hard as shit to say."

Allie took a deep breath and placed her hands over her heart. "I've been seeing someone. He's a nice man. Very handsome, not that you were ever jealous. It's just lonely without you."

Allie grabbed a fistful of grass, threw it with all her might, and the wind blew it back onto her lap.

"Damn it!" Allie screamed.

"We don't say it. I think we both feel it and would mean it if we did, but we don't. I still wear my ring, even when he visits.

"Stan hasn't met him. No one has, really. I slipped him a note in the café, but Wanda's on to us. No secrets with that ole bat. None. Anyway, I wanted you to know. I don't need your permission, but I still wanted you to know."

A truck sped by on its way to someplace. *Any place but here*, Allie thought.

"I need to read his memory, but I couldn't do it alone. He looks so much like you. He shaved last week and used my razor." Allie giggled and snorted. "Our baby shaves. He's been wearing your cologne. Stan is growing up, and I don't even know if he misses you. He was so little."

Allie took the envelope from her bag and held it in her lap. "What if I don't want to hear it? Like you can answer me. This is so stupid. Talking to dirt and ash."

Allie wiped her eyes, squeezed the ring on her left hand between her pointer and thumb like she was popping shipping bubbles, and stared at the envelope. Time slipped from the present into the past, and the wind carried the dust from the cotton fields across the plains. It smelled like dirt and cow shit.

"You would have said that's the smell of money. I would have laughed, and snorted, and told you that money smells pretty damn gross, then."

"God, I miss you so much. Do you know that? Of course, you don't. Or? Maybe you do? I wish I knew."

When Allie looked down at her hands, the college-ruled notebook paper and Stan's meticulous handwriting lay open before her. "Well, I hope you can hear this. Wherever you are, Jimmy McDermitt."

My First Memory
by Stanley McDermitt

The first memory I remember isn't something I remember at all. It is something I wish I could remember. I remember this for my mom. She deserves this memory, so I choose to remember it.

My mom is the most amazing and strongest person I know. She loved my dad so much that she still wears her wedding ring. My first memory of my dad is the day he came home from Iraq. We met him at the airport. It wasn't like the movies. No band played. He didn't appear out of a column of flags in his dress blue uniform.

He was wearing jeans and a T-shirt. It didn't matter to my mom. She left me standing by the airport door, sprinted toward the luggage tram, and jumped into his arms. Her smile was electric.

We had lunch at Outback, and my dad ordered me a steak off the adult menu. It was a big deal. They held hands on the ride home, and she stole kisses when she thought I was sleeping. When we got home, he told me he had a gift for me and told me to meet him in the backyard.

I stood out there waiting, and he came barreling down the steps wearing his baseball glove on his left hand. He walked toward me with his other arm behind his back. Then, he put his glove on top of my head and held out his other hand. It was my very own glove. He asked me to play catch.

We played until the sun went down. That's when I saw Mom sitting at the kitchen table watching us. She flipped on the backyard light. We played catch in the light of our backyard as the stars shone overhead. Momma watched through the window. This morning at breakfast, I almost swore my mom was reliving that day as she looked out at our backyard.

My dad was home, and things were really good. Mom was happy, and Dad seemed very content. I pretended I didn't hear him waking up from his dreams in the night. Mom was worried enough about Dad without adding me to her list of problems. She told me, a part of your dad never came back home, Stan the Man. He wasn't always like this. Mom asked me if I could remember him. You know, before.

That's why my first memory isn't one I really remember, but I wish I did. It would make my mom feel better. The memory I don't have goes like this.

Dad stood at attention in his dress blue uniform. A band was playing, and the airplanes were lined up on the runway behind them. The president was there. He gave a speech about America's heroes. My mom whispered to me, "Stan, your dad is a hero." I was in my stroller and waving a little flag in each hand.

A sergeant yelled at them, and then my dad came over to say goodbye. Dad picked me up, hugged me, kissed my cheek, and said, "Take care of your mom while I'm gone." I saluted and said, "Yes, sir." He kissed Mom goodbye. We watched the plane leave while the band played the fireworks song.

This is my first memory because it just has to be what happened. When I close my eyes and imagine what my three-year-old self had to see, what I had to remember, this is my first memory. See, Mom. I remember him the way you do. The way he was before the dreams, before not being able to sleep or be in a crowd. I remember him the way you need me to, Mom. I remember him. So you can let go now. It's OK. I know he loved you so much because I am his son. I am a little Jimmy McDermitt. You say so all the time.

> *Listen to me, Mom. I know my dad loves you and wants you to be happy because I do, too.*
>
> *This is my first memory. I remember my dad the way he was before whatever happened in that place changed him. I choose to remember him exactly like that. Playing catch while you sit at the table and watch. I remember Dad like he was before. That is my first memory. It's for my mom, Allie McDermitt. The strongest person I know.*

***

It was dusk when her cell phone rang. Allie had the paper in one hand and a clump of grass in the other. She looked at the caller ID; it was Stan.

"Hey, Stan the Man."

"Mom?"

"Yeah, baby. What's up?"

"You working late?"

"Just finishing up a case. I'll be home in a bit."

"What's for supper?"

"Let's go out. I'll pick you up in ten minutes."

"Cool."

Allie brushed off the headstone with one hand and held her phone in the other. Stan's profile photo was on the screen. It was from T-ball. Little Stan was trying his best to look tough, which made every five-year-old look like they were pouting. His glove was on his left hand, and his right hand was fist down in the webbing like Jimmy had taught him to break in a new baseball glove. Jimmy would say, "Spit and hit. Spit and hit. Spit and hit." Give a five-year-old that vernacular gem and see if they ever lose it.

"Mom? You OK?"

"I sure am. Be home in a minute."

"I'll be here. Hungry."

"When are you not?"

"When I'm sleeping, I guess, but sometimes I even dream about eating."

"Of course you do. Be home in a minute."

She hung up and looked back down at Jimmy's headstone.

Allie slipped the gold talisman of eternal commitment off and slid it into the envelope with Stan's writing. She outlined Jimmy's name on the warm white stone with her finger and declared,

"Someday, some woman is going to take this boy from me. She'll be wearing this ring."

Allie got to her feet, and her shadow stretched away from the grave toward the road. Both feet stood firmly in the past, but fate pushed her further into the future with each passing day. In her pocket, she carried two lifeless items, talismans of the past, the present, and the future, bursting at the seams, full of a story only fate could tell.

Allie looked down at Jimmy's resting place and whispered, "Good night, Jimmy. I love you."

Allie made her way back to her car, and a thought sprang forth in her mind as she started it. She reached for her journal, clicked the ballpoint pen into write mode, and wrote.

> *Two youthful dreamers ran as fast as they could away from the town whose charter bore their surnames. One left to learn, the other to fight a war. Four decades lay between each departure, but both shared the same fate. When they returned, except for the changes that time demands, their image in the mirror was unchanged. But, just below each stoic facade were the scars fate left behind. Each returned a shattered shell of the man who had*

left. Each came home carrying a baseball glove.

Allie closed the journal, slid the pen back into its holder, and pressed the hands-free button on her car's steering wheel. "Call Denton Briar."

After one ring, Denton answered. "Allie, are you OK?"

"I'm fine."

"You never call me on a weeknight. You scared me."

"Have you had dinner?"

"No."

"Good. Meet me at the diner. There's someone you need to meet."

The "Welcome to Appleton" sign was in the rearview mirror when Allie broke the silence. "Denton?"

"I'm still here."

"Good, I thought I lost you there for a second."

"Are you sure about this?"

"You'd better hurry up before I change my mind."

"Allie, we don't have to do this until you're sure."

"I'm sure."

"I'll be there in fifteen minutes."

"OK. See you there."

To be continued...

Part Four

1

The parking lot was empty. This was unusual for a Monday night, but then Allie remembered the Cowboys were playing. Though not a fan, she had heard her coworkers talking about the game in the hospital break room. There weren't many things that could cause the day-to-day activities of Appledale to come to a screeching halt, but a high school football game or a Cowboys game sure could.

Allie parked in her choice of spots, looked over at Stan, and divulged, "Stan the Man, a friend of mine is going to meet us for dinner."

"Mom! I thought we had a deal," moaned Stan.

"We do. I don't see any of your friends sitting in the car."

Stan implored, “Please don’t call me that in front of the toothbrush guy.”

“Toothbrush guy?” Allie gasped.

“He left his toothbrush in our bathroom.”

Allie giggled. “Nothing gets past you, does it?”

“When there’s suddenly three toothbrushes instead of two, it’s hard to not notice.”

“I guess so. I want you to know that I love you, and I loved your dad very much.”

“I know, Mom.” Stan looked toward the diner and added, “It’s OK. I want you to be happy, and I know Dad does, too. Can I ask you something?”

“Shoot.”

Stan sputtered, “Was Dad’s car wreck really an accident?”

Tears welled up in her eyes, and she whimpered, “I don’t know. I wish I did, but I don’t.”

Stan leaned across the car, wrapped his arms around his mother, and cried, “Mom, either way, it wasn’t your fault. It wasn’t my fault. What he saw or what he did caused it. So, in a way, it wasn’t his fault, either.”

"I know, baby. He was hurting so bad on the inside. I like to think he's at peace now. I pray he is."

"He is, Mom. I know it."

Allie passed Stan a tissue, and they wiped their eyes. Neither spoke until Denton Briar's headlights illuminated the car's interior as he pulled his old pickup truck into the empty parking space beside them.

Allie opened the car door and said, "All right, Stan the Man, let's do this."

"Mom! Our deal?"

Allie and Stan stood on the curb in front of the neon sign that read "Dixon's Diner." Denton stepped out of his truck and walked over to them.

Allie stood behind Stan with her hands on his shoulders and said, "Denton, I'd like you to meet Stan."

Denton held out his hand and replied, "It's a pleasure to meet you."

Stan shook Denton's hand. "It's nice to meet you, too. You left your toothbrush at our house."

Denton looked at Allie and shrugged his shoulders. "Did I?"

"Sure did," Stan reported. "Let's go. I'm starving!"

The trio entered the café and walked to a table in the back.

Wanda spouted, "Good evening, handsome," as she delivered three sets of silverware wrapped in paper napkins and menus to a table near the window. "I knew you'd leave me for someone younger."

"Well, it was bound to happen," Denton retorted.

Allie, Stan, and Denton looked up at the daily special posted on the chalkboard above the kitchen service window.

Wanda advised, "Sorry, we ran out of coleslaw, but we got the rest of it." She looked down at Stan and laughed. "Not sure I've got enough food to fill his empty pit of a stomach, but we can make a head start."

Allie replied, "That's all any of us can do lately."

"Well, a growing boy needs calories. What are y'all drinking?"

Allie ordered coffee, Denton asked for a beer, and Stan requested a root beer that came in a long-neck bottle, just like a real one. Wanda scurried away to grab the drinks. Allie and Denton studied the day's menu, and Stan opened a cracker package from the condiment tray, which contained assorted jellies, salt and pepper shakers, sugar and sweetener packages, and a squeeze bottle of generic fancy ketchup.

"What makes it fancy ketchup?" asked Stan.

"That's a great question. Denton, why do they call it fancy ketchup?" asked Allie, raising her eyebrows twice.

"Well, Your Honor and members of the jury. Let's first look at the definition of the word 'fancy.'"

"Denton, seriously?" Allie quipped, looking over at Stan, who was waiting to see how far Denton could carry this "fancy" conversation.

"Yes. Seriously. Any question can be deduced by applying logic and common sense."

Allie chuckled. "By all means, don't let us stop you."

Stan stopped nibbling on the crackers and gave Denton his full attention.

"In this situation, I believe the most appropriate definition is the one that defines 'fancy' as something a person wants or, even better, desires. Since I've never met anyone who didn't like ketchup, it's fancy cause we all…wait for it…fancy it."

Wanda arrived with the drinks, set them on the table, and placed her hands on her hips. "Denton, only a lawyer could come up with some bullsh…uhm, crap like that."

Denton looked up at Wanda and probed, "All right then, Wanda. Why is it called fancy ketchup?"

Wanda rolled her eyes, moved her hands from her hips, and rested them on the table. "All three of you are sitting here with the definition and reasoning for everything known to man sitting right here on the table, and you're gonna let this smart…butt lawyer make up some shit?" She looked down at Stan. "Sorry."

"It's all right, Wanda. Mom says that all the time."

Allie spewed her coffee across the table, and a fine mist of buffed leather greatness landed on Denton's and Stan's faces. Wanda laughed so hard that the table shook.

Through tears of laughter, Wanda replied, "From the mouths of babes."

Allie snorted, Stan doubled over and grabbed his shirt, and Denton folded over in a full belly laugh.

When Wanda caught her breath, she continued, "What I was saying before Allie gave you two a coffee shower was that those phones are good for something besides taking naked pictures of yourself and selling them on the internets."

"You can do that?" Stan inquired.

"No, you certainly cannot," Allie refuted.

Wanda pulled her chin down toward her right shoulder and cocked one eyebrow. "You can, but just because you can does not mean you should. You can also use those things to watch videos."

Allie countered, "That's quite enough, Wanda. Stan has learned enough already."

"Allie, what did you think I was going to say? I watch videos of fat people falling on the YouTube. Those are my favorite."

Allie breathed out in relief, and Wanda explained, "You can also find the answer to damn near anything by asking that Serious girl."

"Serious?" probed Stan.

"Yeah. Watch." Wanda pulled the iPhone from her apron pocket and spoke to it. "Hey, Serious. Why is ketchup called fancy?"

Allie, Stan, and Denton's eyes met, and laughter ensued again. Allie snorted. Over "Serious" answering Wanda's question, Wanda implored, "What's so damn funny about that?"

"Serious" continued from the iPhone, "Fancy ketchups are smoother, firmer, largely free of noticeable bits of tomato, and optimally balanced between sweet and sour notes."

Stan replied, "Her name is Siri."

"Seriously?" asked Wanda.

"Seriously," laughed Denton.

Wanda shrugged. "Well, I guess she's polyonymous?"

"What does that even mean?" asked Allie.

"She identifies with different names, just like you, Allie."

"What other name do I identify with?" asked Allie.

"You always answer to smart ass."

Stan took in a deep "oh crap" breath and looked across the table to see exactly how he should respond to this showdown of female alphas. Denton burst into laughter, but Stan held his mouth agape until Allie let out a giggle, and Stan melted into the quartet's uncontrollable frivolity.

Wanda giggled. "What are you having, smart ass?"

The trio placed their dinner order, and Wanda returned to the window to deliver it to the cook. She clipped the order on the metal clip that hung from a silver wire across the service window, looked over her shoulder, and asked Nate, "Would you look at that?"

Nate took the ticket from the clip, looked at the happy trio, and smiled. "Well, I haven't seen a smile like that on Allie McDermitt's face since the day her Jimmy came home from Iraq."

"I know. Makes my heart happy."

"Me, too." Nate looked over the ticket and asked, "That's a lot of food. Someone else joining them?"

"Nope. That boy's twelve."

Nate giggled. "I'll put a little extra on his."

Wanda sat on her stool behind the counter and watched Denton, Allie, and Stan talk, laugh, and not be distracted by an app, a text, or any other technological distraction—three people who needed each other and didn't even know it until they did. Tonight, they began to know.

The food was served, the meal eaten, and Stan ordered pie. Time flew by as fast as it always does when someone wants it to last forever. Wanda entered the kitchen, switched off the lights, and returned to the counter.

"You kids don't have to go home, but I gotta cat that expects me home by ten thirty, or he'll get worried."

"Sorry, Wanda. We're on our way out," Allie replied.

They all said good night, and Wanda locked the door behind them.

The three stood in front of their parked cars.

Denton extended his hand like he was closing a serious negotiation and said, "Stan, this was nice. You're not nearly as mean as your momma says."

Allie elbowed Denton in the ribs and teased, "Denton!"

"It was nice to meet you, too." Stan shook his hand again and then looked at Allie. "I'll go ahead and get in the car so y'all can kiss or whatever."

Allie and Denton embraced and kissed good-night.

"Allie, you know that thing we're not going to say?"

"Yes."

"Well, I'm not going to say it, but I mean it."

Allie smiled and kissed the tip of his nose. "So do I."

2

The sky was partly cloudy, and the stars peeked in and out of heaven's curtains, racing southeast across the Texas plains. Mr. Morton sat in the garden with Lacy asleep at his feet. She was chasing squirrels again, and, in a way, so was Mr. Morton. The debate raged in his mind. He knew he needed to tell her before she found out on her own. It was only a matter of time before everyone in Appledale would know his fate.

He looked down at the sleeping dog. "I'm going to have to share this with all three of the women in my life. Might as well start with you."

The old black dog raised her snow-flecked muzzle and looked as if she already knew. She got up slowly and lay her head in Mr. Morton's lap.

"Looks like my forgetfulness is a little more than old age, sweetheart."

Mr. Morton rubbed Lacy's floppy ears and whispered, "You're taking this better than Wanda will. Will you sit here with me while I call her?"

Lacy rubbed her head against Mr. Morton's thigh. He opened his flip phone and dialed Wanda.

Wanda answered on the first ring. "Lee, you horny old goat. It's eleven o'clock on a Monday night."

Mr. Morton chuckled. "Well, if you're offering?"

"I am not, but I'm not saying I wouldn't, either."

Mr. Morton asked, "Can you come over?"

"Sure, I can. Everything OK?"

"Things are fine, sweety. Could use some company tonight, is all."

"OK. Open the barn so people won't see my car."

"You park right out front."

"Seriously?"

"Uh-huh, we have been loving each other for what, fifteen years? Who gives a shit what anyone thinks?"

"Lee Morton, you're scaring me. You just said 'shit.' Everything OK?"

"Yeah, I'll see you in a few. I'm out back in the garden."

"I'll be there in ten."

"OK."

Mr. Morton rubbed Lacy's head and warned, "She's going to take this hard, so I'm going to need your help. You OK with that?"

Lacy didn't answer, but Mr. Morton knew she would by just being there. She always did.

3

The next morning's brilliant sunrise shone through Mr. Morton's bedroom window. Wanda rolled over. Mr. Morton wasn't there. She found him sitting in his chair, dressed for work, staring intently at the baseball glove on the mantel.

"Lee, let's get you going. You're going to be late for school."

"I called in today. Do you think I'll forget how much hope that old glove held, how much heartbreak it stores?"

"Lee, let's not focus on that. Let's focus on living. Now, come on. You're going to work."

"Wanda, I should have married you."

"Well, Lee Morton, all you had to do was ask."

Mr. Morton walked across the room. “I don’t have a ring, but…”

“We can go shopping this afternoon. I’m not worried about that.”

Mr. Morton knelt and kissed Wanda’s left hand. “Wanda Dixon, will you marry me?”

Tears rolled down Wanda’s cheeks; she went down on one knee, met Mr. Morton’s gaze eye to eye, and chuckled. “I thought you’d never ask.”

The two familiar lovers hugged in a programmed way, but it was different now. Each sensed the hesitancy of commitment and the shame of illegitimacy lift their heavy loads. They sank into the warmth of the love that had always been there. Except now, there were no strings, no guilt, and best of all, no secrets.

Mr. Morton led his fiancée into the kitchen and pulled the dining room chair out for her. He grabbed two coffee cups, filled them at the coffee maker, and sat across from her.

“I’m going to need a lawyer. Any suggestions?” asked Mr. Morton.

Wanda scratched her head and answered, “Only one I can think of. Do you know Denton Briar?”

"Not well."

"He must be a good guy, or Allie McDermitt wouldn't be hanging around with him."

A gracious smile spread across Mr. Morton's face. "I'm so glad she is opening herself up to love again. After Anne died, falling in love again never crossed my mind. Then, I met you."

Mr. Morton reached his hand across the table. Wanda met him halfway. They rubbed each other's hands with their thumbs like nervous teenagers too damn happy to sit still.

"I want to update my will while I'm still of sound mind and body."

"Listen here, Lee Morton, I am not marrying you for the money. I got plenty of my own. So, don't go thinking you're leaving all this land to me."

Mr. Morton released her hand, sat back, and crossed his arms. "That wasn't exactly what I had in mind, either."

"Well, good! I'm no charity case."

"You ever met someone and knew they were meant to do something great? I mean, change-the-world great."

"Yeah, he's sitting right in front of me."

"That's not what I meant."

"I know it, but you need to hear this. For four decades, you have given hope and spurred the imaginations of thousands of young people in this little town, inspiring them to live beyond its expectations. Nothing in my book is greater than that, Lee."

"It's nice of you to say."

"I ain't saying it to be nice. It's the truth. You have changed lives. Do you know Allie comes in every morning, takes her coffee, and writes in her little brown book?" Wanda looked down at the table and quivered. "I think those stories in that book are what kept her alive after Jimmy died. Those stories came from your teaching. That's the difference you've made. That's a real change in the world. You did that."

Mr. Morton took a sip of his coffee and set it back down. "I can't take credit for her gift. She had that the first time I read what she put down on paper. I'll admit I helped her find her voice. That's all I can take credit for."

"You sell yourself short. Sometimes, all a person needs is a dream and someone to encourage it to fruition. That encouragement, and shaping, and honing of skills can only be done by a master teacher. Which you arc."

"I don't know about that."

"I do, and before this horrible disease robs you of clarity, I'm gonna make sure you see the impact you've had."

"Listen to me, Wanda. Don't assume I've already lost my mind because, on this, I am crystal clear."

"I'm listening."

"Allie McDermitt was born with a story to tell. It's a dream I mean to give her the means to achieve."

"How are you going to do that?"

"Do you have any idea how much my land is worth?"

"Not a clue."

"Enough money that Allie can work on her writing full time for the rest of her life and give Stan the attention a boy without a father needs."

"I don't think he'll be without a father figure."

"Really?"

"Really. That lawyer I mentioned got introduced to Stan last night at the café."

Rays of contentment shone through Mr. Morton's eyes, and a sliver of understanding came over Wanda.

"You mean to leave it to her, don't you?"

"Part of it."

"Why not all?"

"Because every kid in this town deserves the opportunity to dream their dreams, too. Eighty percent will be held in a trust, the interest of which will fund full tuition scholarships for every kid that graduates from Appledale."

"Jesus, Lee. How much money are you talking about? A million?"

Mr. Morton shook his head no.

"Ten?"

No response.

"Fifteen?"

Mr. Morton pointed upward.

"I give up, Lee. I can't think in numbers that big."

Mr. Morton laughed. "I can't, either. That's why I put it away a long time ago."

He explained, "When my parents died, I was their only child. The years during World War II were good for cotton. Dad just put that money away for the lean years. That interest added up over the decades, and he never really spent much money. He always had the mindset he was penniless and was so afraid of going broke, he stretched every dollar.

"I've never touched that money. I lease fifteen hundred acres to a commercial farming outfit. I've never spent any of that, either. The land is prime farmland. It should bring around twenty thousand an acre. Plus, the twenty-five million stashed away for a rainy day brings it to—"

"Holy shit," Wanda interrupted. "That's over forty million dollars."

"Give or take a few million."

"Have you shared this with Allie?"

"No. I don't want you to, either. She needs to know I'm sick but can't know about the rest until I'm gone."

"If that's the way you want it."

"That's the way I want it."

"Maybe using Denton for this isn't the best idea, then."

Mr. Morton scratched the white whiskers on his chin. "Allie is an astute judge of character. If she trusts that man enough to meet Stan, I'm not worried about him."

"Forty-five million dollars can turn an honest man bad. You need to think about this."

Mr. Morton breathed in and smirked. "You haven't changed your mind yet?"

"About what?"

"Marrying me?"

"Nope, but I know how big the diamond better be."

Laughter filled the kitchen. Two worn hearts beat longingly toward a fate that neither imagined nor could have written on their own. Allie and Stan's lives would never again have the burden of finance crushing their dreams in its wake. The children of Appledale would have a means to explore their passions into perpetuity.

Mr. Morton's worn brown leather shoes sat alone beside the floormat that read "Welcome." His late wife had given them to him on his first day of school, and he'd worn them on every first day since. They would not see another first day, but he wore them again on his last.

4

The master teacher left Appledale Junior High School the same way he entered it four decades before: full of hope, wonder, and excitement, tinged with a pinch of sadness. Mr. Morton walked down the steps by the flagpole and didn't look back. He knew the memories of that place, this life, and the people he encountered along the way would fade, but even in the sorrow, he found hope. Lee would mourn this career, but not for long. He was scheduled to begin work at the diner the next day.

A tear rolled down his cheek as he slid into Wanda's car. She leaned over, kissed him, and winked. "Mr. Morton, can I buy you dinner? I know a great place." She put the car in drive. "The food is great, but the waitress is a mean ole bitch."

“She tries to be.”

“What do you mean, ‘tries’?”

“You know exactly what I mean, Mrs. Morton. Everyone knows you’re a softy.”

“Shush, now. Don’t go telling people that. It’ll ruin my reputation.”

The unbelievably large diamond caught the afternoon sun, and a prism of light reflected on Wanda’s face as she drove toward the town square and Dixon’s Diner. The parking lot was full except for a spot directly in front of the café, reserved by an orange traffic cone. A banner hung over the diner’s sign that read “Thank you, Mr. Morton.”

Allie and Stan moved the traffic cone onto the sidewalk, and Wanda and Mr. Morton parked in their reserved spot for his special day.

“Oh, Wanda. You didn’t have to do this.”

“I didn’t do it. This was all Allie.”

“Who’s Allie?”

“You know, Allie. You’ve been helping her with her writing.”

“I had a student named Alice Henderson. I think she went by Allie.”

Wanda reached across the console and patted Mr. Morton's knee. "That's her. It's Allie McDermitt now."

"So, she and Jimmy got married?"

"They sure did."

"I remember now. Their boy, Stan, is in my class."

"Sure is. That's her and Stan waiting on the sidewalk."

"This is so nice. Thank you."

"Don't thank me. Tonight is all about thanking you."

"For what?"

"For just being you."

Mr. and Mrs. Morton walked into the diner, holding hands.

So many people were at the café that tables were set out on the sidewalks and in the alley behind. Student after student came by Mr. Morton's table. He didn't remember every name, but Lee Morton made sure each person experienced his gratitude.

The sun's tangerine rays splashed below the horizon on that chilly December day in the tiny town of Appledale, Texas. The old rock courthouse's shadow lay across the parking lot in the light of a full winter's moon. Life would go on in Appledale, as life does. The actors would make their entrances and their exits. Mr. Morton's exit was beautiful, sad, and joyous all at the same time. The tales of their lives played out on the stage where fate had placed them, writing their stories between the curtains. A story only fate could tell.

The End

www.ingramcontent.com/pod-product-compliance
Lightning Source LLC
LaVergne TN
LVHW090527110826
845146LV00003B/1009

* 9 7 9 8 9 9 5 9 7 1 7 0 2 *